P9-BJD-902

25

DISCARD

12

MIRROR MIRROR

Dee Phillips

4/19/15 $15 Follet Pell Ac

RiGHT NOW!

Blast	Goal
Dare	Goodbye
Dumped	Grind
Eject	Joyride
Fight	**Mirror**
Friends?	Scout

First published by Evans Brothers Limited

2A Portman Mansions, Chiltern Street, London W1U 6NR, United Kingdom

Copyright © Ruby Tuesday Books Limited 2010

This edition published under license from Evans Limited

SADDLEBACK
P U B L I S H I N G
www.sdlback.com

© 2014 by Saddleback Educational Publishing

ISBN-13: 978-1-62250-879-2
ISBN-10: 1-62250-879-3
eBook: 978-1-63078-014-2

Printed in Guangzhou, China
NOR/0114/CA21400044

18 17 16 15 14   1 2 3 4 5

I look in the mirror.

Skinny. Ugly.

At least I can't see how short I am.

I look in the mirror.

Skinny.

Ugly.

I want to look like David Beckham.
I want to look like Cristiano Ronaldo.

At least I can't see how short I am.

I wanted to play well today.
So I read this stuff online.

Go for it!
Hold your head up!

Yeah,
right!

I went for it.

And I missed an open goal.

I held my head up.

And I fell over.

Mom taps on my door.
She says, "I got the stuff you wanted."
I look at the body spray and DVD.
I think about the TV ads.

I think, "You're a skinny,
ugly freak, Will Jones."

I look in the mirror.

Fat.

Ugly.

I want to look like Selena Gomez.
I want to look like Taylor Swift.

At least red hair doesn't
show in the dark.

I wanted to look good tonight.
I hardly ate anything all week.

I spent money on makeup and a fake tan.

Yeah, right!

No chocolate all week.
But my new jeans were still too tight.

A new tan and makeup.
But I still looked ugly.

13

I sat in the corner all night.

No one talked to me.

I want to be thin and pretty.
Then everybody would talk to me.

I say, "You're a fat, ugly freak,
Brenna Owen."

17

It's Monday. We've got art.
I'm working on my project.

Miss Allen says, "This looks amazing, Will."
She says, "You should enter the design
contest."

I look at the screen.
I turn bright red.
I say, "Thanks, Miss Allen.
But I don't think so."

That night I watch my soccer DVD.
I look in the mirror.

Skinny.

Short.

Bad at sports.

I'm worthless.

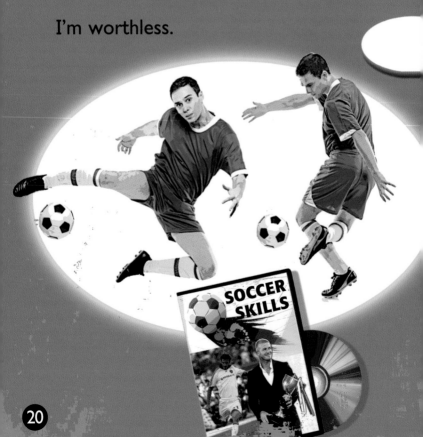

It's Monday. I'm looking at the bulletin board.

Mr. King says, "You should try out for the show, Brenna. You're a good singer."

I turn bright red.
I say, "Thanks, Mr. King.
But I don't think so."

That night I look in the mirror.

Fat.

Ugly.

Red hair.

I wish I was thin with dark hair.
Then I could try out for the show.

It's Friday. Lunchtime.
I go to the art room.

Brenna Owen is working
on her project.
She doesn't see me come in.

I like Brenna.
She's funny and kind.

Brenna is singing to herself.
She's a great singer.

I say, "Hi, Brenna."

She stops singing
and turns bright red.

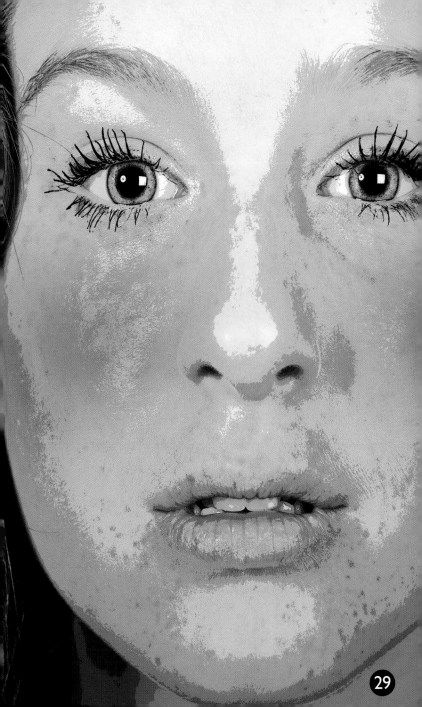

Oh no!
Will Jones just heard me singing.
I was working on my project.
I didn't see him come in.
He said hi. Then he turned bright red.

I like Will.
He has cool ideas.
I must look at his project.
I bet it's amazing!

31

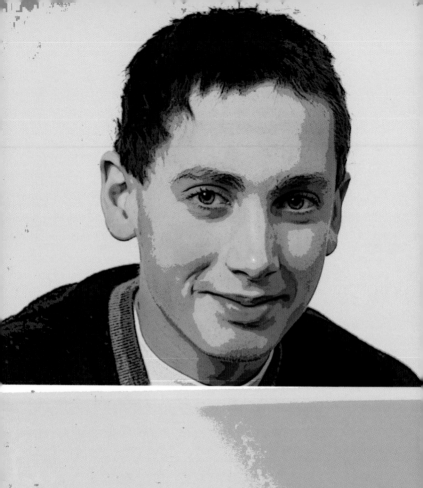

Brenna comes over.
She looks at my project.

She says, "Wow. That looks great.
My dad's a designer. He would give
you a job in a heartbeat."

What is Beauty?

Then Brenna looks sad.

She says, "I wish I looked like those girls."

I say, "It's all done on the computer, Brenna."

I make the girl look thinner.

I give her an instant tan.

I look at Will's screen.
He says, "You're a really good singer.
You should try out for the show."

I say, "I don't look right."

Will holds up his phone.
I laugh.
I say, "Don't, Will!"

A minute later I'm on the computer screen.

I look at the screen.

I say, "Wow. What did you do, Will?"

He says, "Nothing, Brenna.
It's all you."

I sit next to Will.
I feel so happy.
I say, "You have cool ideas.
You should enter that design contest."

Brenna gives me a big smile.
I smile back.
I say, "Maybe I will!"

GO FOR IT
ON YOUR OWN

Will won't enter a design contest because he doesn't play soccer well.

Brenna won't try out as a singer in the show because she has red hair.

Think of something you are good at.
What could you do with this skill?
Why aren't you doing it?
Does your reason make sense?

Set a goal for yourself, and go for it!

MIRRORS
WITH A PARTNER

Brenna and Will describe themselves as skinny, short, fat, and red-headed. They describe each other as funny, kind, and cool.

Fat
Short
Glasses
Freckles
Pale

Funny
Cute
Loyal
Cool
Smiley

• Look in a mirror. Write down five words to describe what you see.

• Ask your partner to write down five words they would use to describe you.

• Compare the two lists. Do friends make good mirrors?

WALLFLOWERS
IN A GROUP

"Wallflowers" cling to the wall at parties! Look at pages 14 and 15. Role-play the scene at the party. Give the guests names and think about their characters. What do the guests think about Brenna?

- She's shy/boring.
- She thinks she's too good for us.
- She looks miserable.
- I didn't notice her!

What does Brenna think?

AD LAND
ON YOUR OWN / WITH A PARTNER / IN A GROUP

Look at pages 8 to 9. The ad is saying:
If you use this spray, girls will want to be with you.
The DVD cover is saying:
If you watch this DVD, you will play like David Beckham.

Find an ad and answer these questions:

- What is it selling?
  What is it saying?
- How realistic is this message?
  (Will the spray attract girls? Will watching a DVD make you a great soccer player?)

IF YOU ENJOYED THIS BOOK, TRY THESE OTHER **RiGHT NOW!** BOOKS.

Alisha's online messages to new girl Sam get nastier and nastier. Will anyone help Sam

Eric's fighter jet is under attack. There's only one way to escape ...

Laci and Jaden were in love, but now it's over. So why is Jaden always watching her?

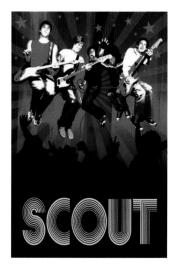

It's Saturday night.
Two angry guys. Two knives.
There's going to be a fight.

Tonight is the band's big
chance. Tonight, a record
company scout is at their gig!

Damien's platoon is under
attack. Another soldier is in
danger. Damien must risk his
own life to save him.

It's just an old, empty house.
Kristi must spend the night
inside. Just Kristi and
the ghost ...

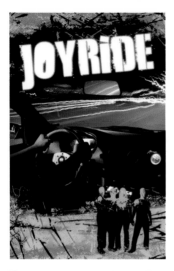

Tanner sees the red car. The keys are inside. Tanner says to Jacob, Bailey, and Hannah, "Want to go for a drive?"

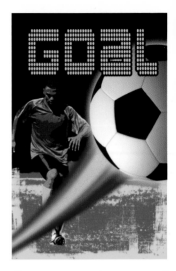

Today is Carlos's tryout with Chivas. There's just one place up for grabs. But today, everything is going wrong!

Taylor hates this new town. She misses her friends. There's nowhere to skate!

Tonight, Kayla must make a choice. Stay in Philadelphia with her boyfriend, Ryan. Or start a new life in California.